A GOLDEN BOOK • NEW YORK

randomhousekids.com

ISBN 978-0-7364-3698-4

MANUFACTURED IN CHINA

10 9 8 7 6 5 4

STAR WARS™

a Little Golden Book®
Collection

HEROES
& VILLAINS

A GOLDEN BOOK • NEW YORK

CONTENTS

I AM A DROID

I am a droid.

I am built to do a special job.

Some droids are **small**.

Some droids are
BIG.

5

Some

droids

walk. . .

some droids **roll**. . .

and some droids *fly*!

Astromech

droids like R2-D2

repair starships

and starfighters.

Beep-
bop-
booP!

They also help pilots navigate
a course through the stars...

Protocol droids like C-3PO are programmed to understand millions of different languages.

They help aliens from strange
planets talk to each other.

Some droids are built to fight!
Battle droids, **super battle droids**,
and **destroyer droids** help armies
win battles.

Zap! Zap!

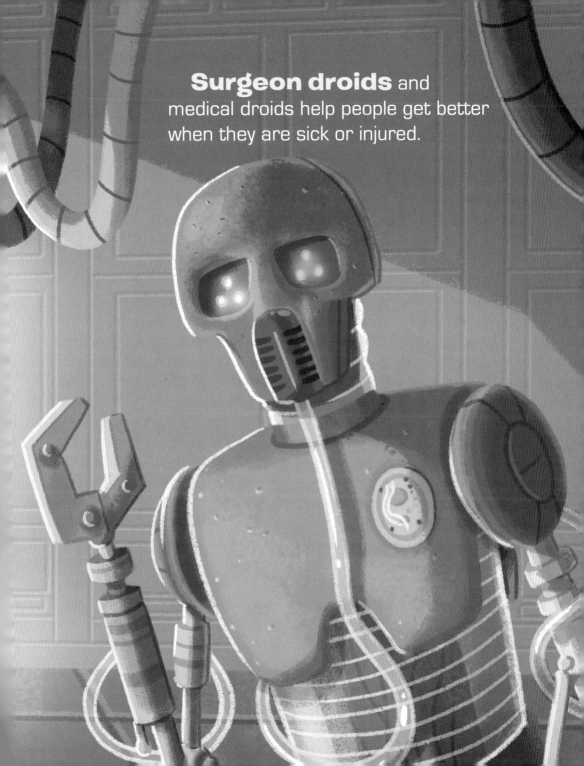

Surgeon droids and medical droids help people get better when they are sick or injured.

Some droids are **bounty hunters**.
IG-88 and 4-LOM track down humans and
aliens who are on the run.

Probe droids are spies!

They report **secret** information to their masters.

Some droids are built to protect.
MagnaGuard droids help keep
General Grievous safe from his enemies.

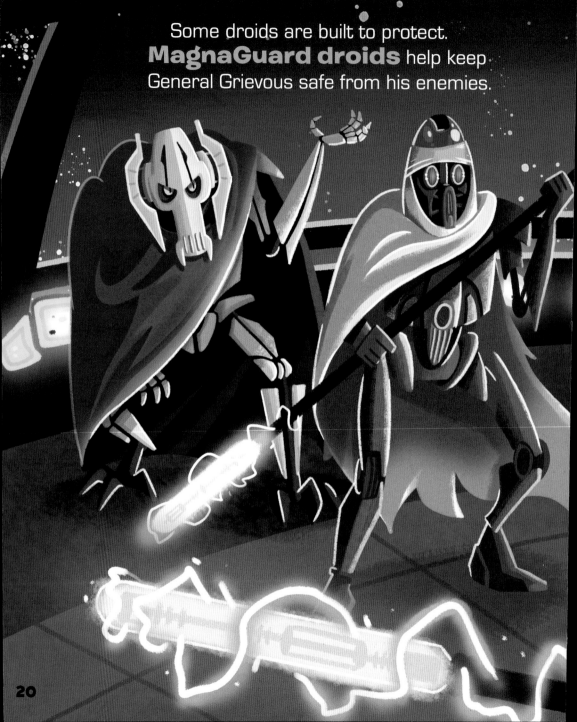

Power droids are like big walking batteries!

Some droids aren't very nice.

But some droids are **heroes**!

I AM A HERO

I am a hero.

I fight for what's right
to help others.

A hero **protects** those
who can't fight for themselves.

Sometimes a hero must fight
for an **entire galaxy** . . .

or just one **tiny** droid.

No battle is too big—or too small—for a true hero.

Heroes will always put the
safety of others before
their own.

Nothing will stop a hero from racing
into danger to **help** someone in need.

Some heroes are **BIG** . . .

and some heroes are **small**.

Some heroes are **old** . . .

and some heroes are
young.

A hero can be a brave **Jedi Knight** . . .

34

or a **queen** . . .

or a **princess** . . .

or a **farm boy** . . .

or a **junk collector**.

Some heroes are **pilots** . . .

and some heroes are **copilots**.

Some heroes are **aliens** . . .

and some heroes are **droids**.

A hero can be
a **father** . . .

or a **son**.

A hero will always be there to offer a **helping hand** . . .

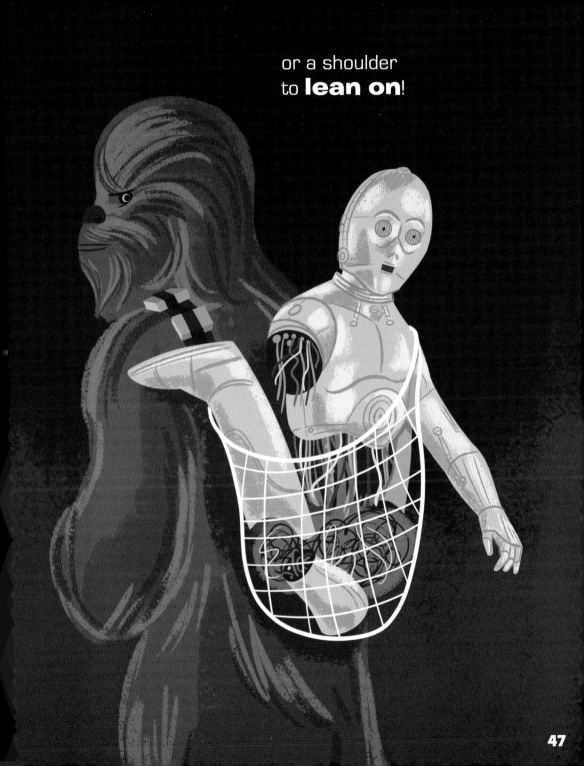

or a shoulder
to **lean on**!

Whether young or old, big or small,
alien or droid—every hero's greatest
strength comes from the **heart**.

I am a Jedi.

I am a guardian who fights for peace and justice.

A Jedi's power comes from the **Force**, an energy field created by all living things that binds the galaxy together.

A Jedi can use the Force to

levitate objects . . .

leap **FAR** . . .

run **FAST** .

jump **HIGH** . . .

trick the weak-minded . . .

and **influence** others!

A Jedi wears
a hooded **cloak**.

Some
Jedi are
big.

Some Jedi are **small**.

Size matters not.

A Jedi's weapon is
the **lightsaber**.

It is a powerful **laser** sword that can cut through anything.

A young Jedi in training
is called a **Padawan**.

Before becoming a Jedi Knight,
a Padawan must be taught by a Jedi
Master in the ways of the **Force**.

A Jedi should
always be at **peace**.
Fighting is the
last resort.

Hate and fear can lead a Jedi down the
path to the **dark side** of the Force.

Anakin Skywalker was once a powerful Jedi who gave in to the dark side.

He became
Darth Vader—

Lord
of
the Sith.

The Sith are **the enemy** of the Jedi. They are evil warriors who use the Force to spread fear.

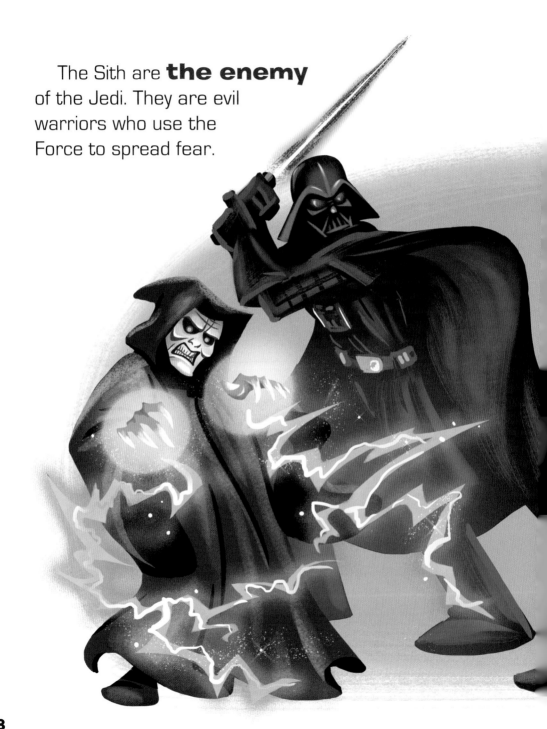

There can be only two Sith Lords at a time—a master and an apprentice.

The Jedi are in a constant **battle** with the Sith to restore balance to the Force.

At the end of
their lives, all Jedi
become one with
the Force.

Some continue to communicate
with the living as **Force Spirits**!

Would **YOU** like to be a Jedi?

I am a pilot.

I fly starships.

Some pilots fly **BIG** starships.

Some pilots fly
small starships.

Some pilots are **young**.

Some pilots

have been flying

for **ages**.

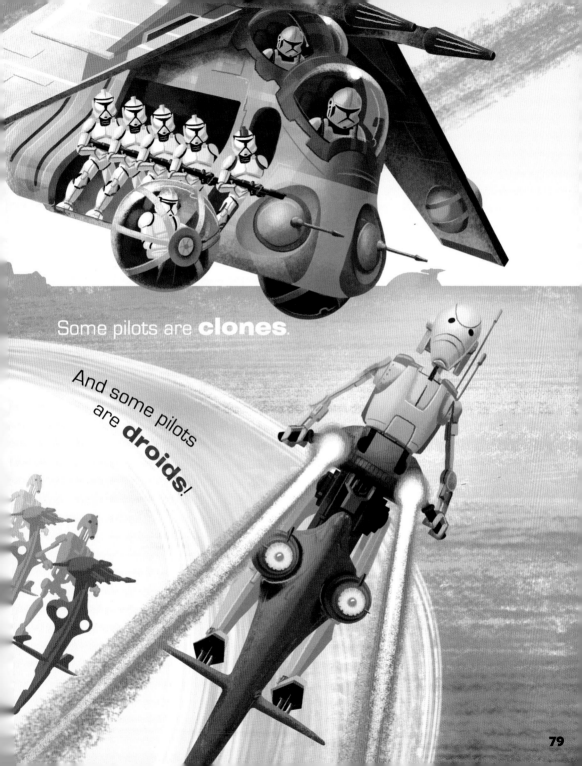

Some pilots are **clones**.

And some pilots
are **droids**!

Some pilots fly for money. Before becoming a hero for the Rebel Alliance, Han Solo delivered special cargo for anyone willing to pay him—even GANGSTERS!

Some pilots like to **race**!

Young Anakin Skywalker
was the

fastest

podracer pilot
on planet Tatooine.

Some pilots fly kings—
and **queens**—
to exotic planets!

Brave pilots fly starfighters on special missions. **X-wing**, **Y-wing**, and **A-wing** pilots helped destroy the Death Star above planet Endor—and defeated the evil Empire once and for all!

Many Jedi Knights are great pilots.

The Force helps them sense
what is ahead—before they can see it!

Every pilot needs a good starship.
The **_Millennium Falcon_** is
Han Solo's pride and joy. It is the
fastest ship in the galaxy.

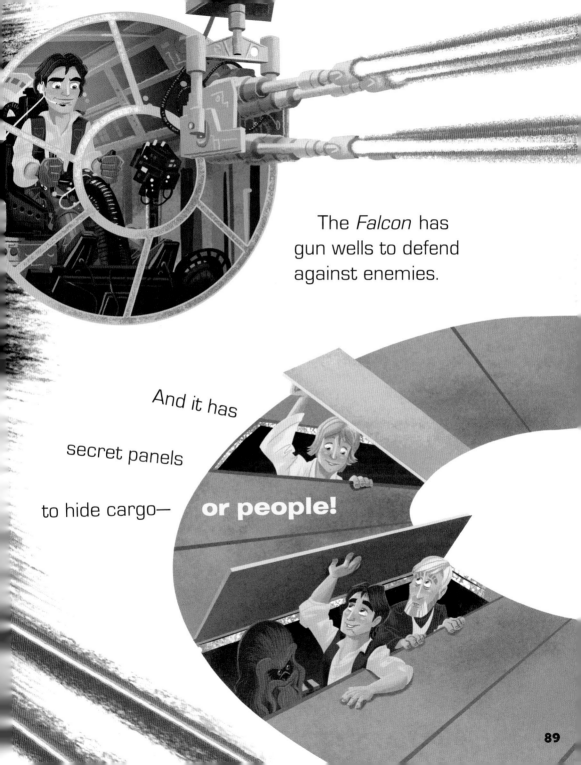

The *Falcon* has gun wells to defend against enemies.

And it has

secret panels

to hide cargo—

or people!

Every pilot needs a good **copilot**.

Han Solo never flies anywhere
without his best friend and partner,

Chewbacca the Wookiee.

Some copilots are droids!
Poe Dameron relies on **BB-8**
to help navigate and keep his
X-wing fighter flying smoothly.

Nien Numb was at Lando Calrissian's side when the Rebel Fleet flew into the Death Star—and blew it up!

BOOM!

Some pilots aren't **very nice!**

Darth Vader and his
Imperial TIE fighter
squadron destroyed many
rebel starships.

There are many different kinds of pilots . . .
but they all **love to fly**!

I AM A PRINCESS

I am a princess.
I lead others and keep them safe.

A princess is the daughter of a royal family. Princess Leia's mother was a wise and brave queen named **Padmé Amidala**. Her father, **Anakin Skywalker**, was a powerful Jedi Knight—a guardian of peace.

But Leia only ever knew her adoptive parents, Senator **Bail Organa** and his wife, **Breha**.

Like her parents, Leia has an **adventurous spirit** and a strong desire for justice.

A princess will do anything to **protect** her people. When the galaxy was in the grips of the evil Empire, Princess Leia joined the rebellion to fight for what's right.

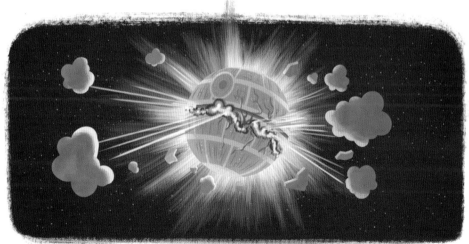

Leia delivered the Death Star plans to the rebels—and **helped** destroy the Empire's gigantic battle station!

A princess must **stand up** to her enemies . . .

no matter how **BIG** and **MEAN** they are!

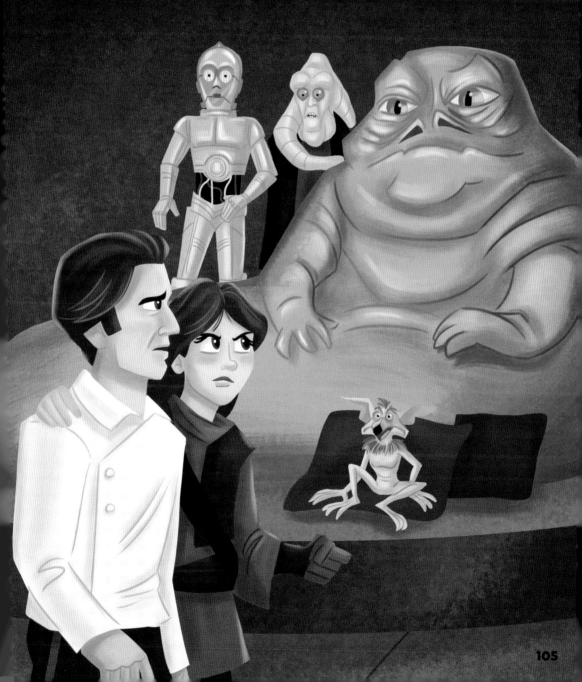

A princess must be ready to **take charge** in any situation . . .

. . . and **race** into action!

A princess is an ambassador of **peace** and goodwill. She makes new friends—and allies—wherever she goes!

Sometimes a princess may find herself in a **scary** place . . .

. . . or a **tight spot**. A princess must always be brave.

Sometimes a princess needs to be **SNEAKY** to outsmart her foes. When rebel hero **Han Solo** was captured and frozen in carbonite, Leia disguised herself as a bounty hunter to rescue him.

From the moment she is born, a princess **devotes** herself to the well-being of others.

A princess must **always** be a hero.

Are you ready to be a **hero**?

I am a Sith.

I am a master of evil.

Sith are **dark warriors** who crave power. They spread fear and try to enslave all those around them.

A Sith's evil power comes from the dark side of the **Force**—an energy field that has been twisted by anger and hate.

Sith can use the dark side to attack their enemies . . .

. . . and create lightning from their fingertips!

Every Sith has a **lightsaber**—a powerful
laser sword that can cut through anything!

Slash!

The energy blade of a Sith lightsaber is always **red**.

The Sith are masters of trickery and lies. Darth Sidious concocted a war to create his own **clone army**.

He took control of the Galactic Republic—
and declared himself the **Emperor**!

Sith are the sworn enemies of the **Jedi Knights**, guardians of peace.

After the Clone Wars, the Sith sent out special agents—called **Inquisitors**—to find and eliminate every Jedi in the galaxy!

Throughout the ages, there have been many **dark-side warriors**. But not all of them have been true Sith.

There can only be two Sith at one time—
a **master** and an **apprentice**. One to
embody power, and the other to crave it.

Darth Maul was the first apprentice to Darth Sidious.

Piloting his **Sith Interceptor**, Darth Maul traveled throughout the galaxy to do his master's evil bidding.

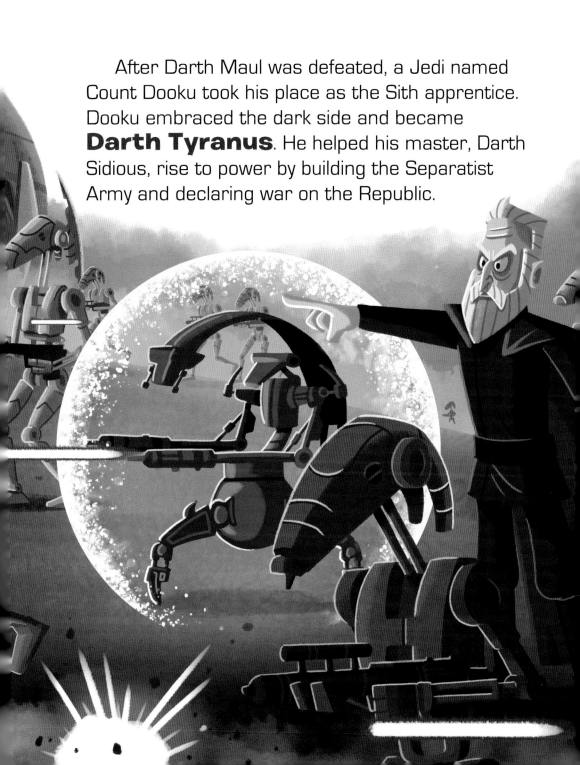

After Darth Maul was defeated, a Jedi named Count Dooku took his place as the Sith apprentice. Dooku embraced the dark side and became **Darth Tyranus**. He helped his master, Darth Sidious, rise to power by building the Separatist Army and declaring war on the Republic.

But Darth Sidious's most powerful Sith apprentice, by light-years, was . . . **Darth Vader**! With Vader by his side, Darth Sidious formed the Galactic Empire and took control of the galaxy.

Darth Vader was once a Jedi Knight named **Anakin Skywalker**. Darth Sidious preyed upon Anakin's fears with lies and tricked him into joining the dark side. Anakin betrayed his master, **Obi-Wan Kenobi**—and the entire Jedi Order!

Darth Vader escaped the evil clutches of the dark side. He was **redeemed** when he saved his son, Luke Skywalker, from Darth Sidious.

Vader destroyed the Emperor and brought peace to the galaxy. The dark side of the Force was gone forever. **Or was it . . . ?**

I AM A STORMTROOPER

I am a stormtrooper.

I am a soldier who fights for the evil First Order. The First Order is trying to defeat the **Resistance** and take control of the galaxy.

Before the rise of the First Order, stormtroopers fought for the **Galactic Empire** against the brave **Rebel Alliance**.

And before the Empire,
stormtroopers were **clones**!

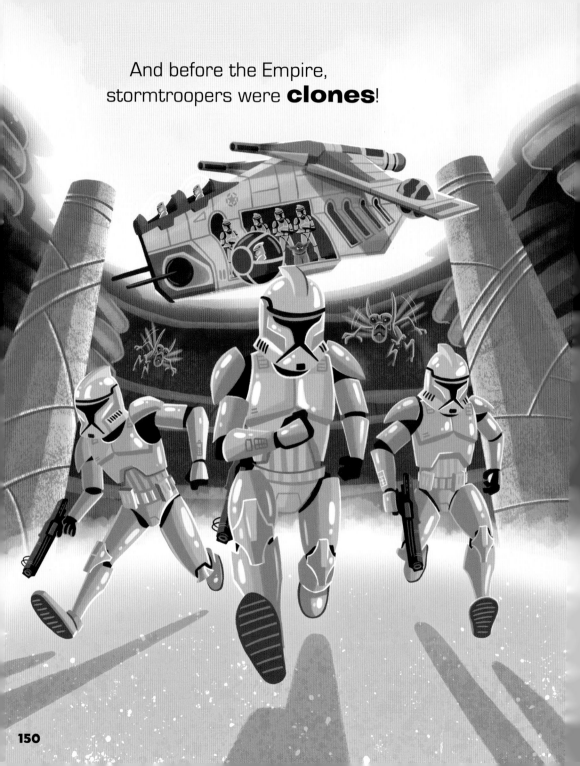

Clone troopers were cloned from a ruthless bounty hunter named **Jango Fett**.

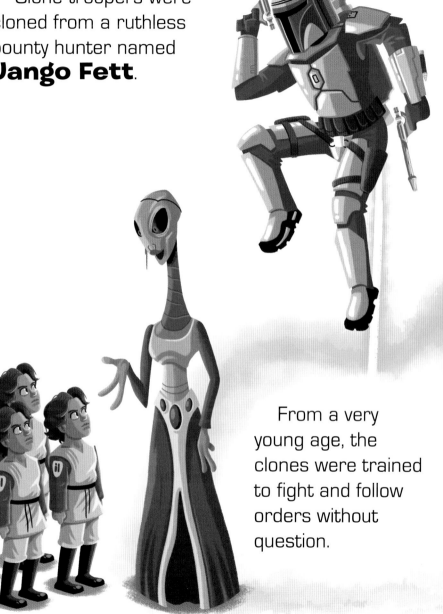

From a very young age, the clones were trained to fight and follow orders without question.

All stormtroopers wear special **armor** to protect them.

There are many different
kinds of stormtroopers.

Snowtroopers are
trained to fight in cold climates.

Sandtroopers are
deployed to hot desert planets.

Scout troopers spy on their
enemies—then zoom away on speeder bikes!

Flametroopers
like to heat things up!

WHOOSH!

Some stormtroopers are pilots who fly **TIE fighters** in epic space battles.

Some stormtroopers are women.

Captain Phasma is an officer in the First Order who commands the respect of her squadrons—and instills fear in her enemies!

Many stormtroopers are **weak-minded**.

They can be easily influenced by others.

But some stormtroopers have a mind of their own.

FN-2187 didn't believe in what he was fighting for.

He fled from the
evil First Order . . .

. . . and became a **hero** of the Resistance!